COWBOY'S CHRISTMAS BLESSING:
Rescued by the Cowboy at Christmas
Book 2

(Sweet Clean Christian Western Romance)
By J. A. Somers

Cowboy's Christmas Blessing

Rescued by the Cowboy at Christmas, Volume 2

J. A. Somers

Published by J. A. Somers, 2022.

Table of Contents

Rescued by the Cowboy at Christmas
Cowboy under the Mistletoe - Book 1
Cowboy's Christmas Blessing - Book 2
Cowboy for Christmas – Book 3
Cowboy's Christmas Wish – Book 4

COWBOY'S CHRISTMAS BLESSING

Evan Charming is one cowboy who isn't looking for love again. He'd lost his wife in a tragic accident. He is determined to never fall in love again—and to never celebrate the holidays.

Gwen Cameron has a lot on her plate. Always trying to prove herself. She doesn't have a lot of luck with relationships. Her ex left her for her best friend. Still, this Christmas, after taking over her late father's tow-truck business, she decides to bury herself in her work. But meeting a tall handsome cowboy may change her plans.

Can two lost souls unite in the spirit of Christmas?

Chapter 1

"Life is a blessing. It's an adventure. You're supposed to *live* it. Isn't that what you and Rhonda used to say?" Evan Charming's brother Cameron said.

The two brothers strung up decorations around the Barn Hall at Charming Ranch for their upcoming annual Christmas celebration. The Charming's Ranch and Resort hosted Christmas for many deserving families around the holidays.

Their mother, a widow and part time matchmaker at the Mistletoe Church, always made sure to keep up the tradition their father and grandfather started many years ago.

She was especially protective of her many sons and nephews and let them know her wishes for them to be happily married—again. She wanted nothing more than to see them happy and to have the ranch filled with grandkids.

Cameron also lost his wife and stepdaughter in a fire. He'd closed himself off from doing fun things in life since then. Cameron was coming around a bit now, but he was always the encourager in the family—anything to take his mind off his own sorrow.

Evan was there for his brother back then when it had happened. It seemed like they all had only each other to rely on.

With the rows of holiday lights strung up outside and garlands inside the newly renovated barn-turned-event hall, it was supposed to put everyone in the festive mood, but right now, Evan felt anything but festive.

He was glad his other brother Noel met his match and was happily married now. But would it ever happen for Evan—again?

He knew he was blessed but sometimes he found it hard to count his blessings after Rhonda went to be with the Lord.

"I'm just not interested in any more adventures," Evan replied. "They're too dangerous."

"Says the cowboy who never passed up an opportunity to stare danger in the face."

This time of the year brought nothing but dread over Evan. He knew he should be celebrating the holidays with his family.

"It's the anniversary. You know how I feel."

Cameron's face fell. "I'm really sorry, bro. I know it must be hard on you. But I just don't want to see you lose yourself. Rhonda would have wanted you to move forward. She wouldn't want you to stop living."

"I know. I thought she was one of my biggest blessings."

"She was."

"But she's no longer with me. I feel as if I'm..."

"Don't say it, man."

"You know what I mean. I think there's one special soul mate for everyone and she was it."

"Have you tried going out on a date? What about the women's ministry?"

"No, thanks. Mom's being trying to hook me up with someone's niece."

"You too, huh?" Cameron chuckled.

He appreciated his brother trying to lift his spirits. But it was no use. His chance had come and gone. His late wife was his chance. That was it. He was determined to go it alone from this time forward. He might be one tough cowboy, but his heart couldn't take any more heartbreak.

Actually, Evan lit a candle for his late wife—every month since her passing.

It wasn't just sorrow. It was guilt. Yes, guilt that washed over him each and every single day.

Why, oh, why didn't he dissuade Rhonda from going on that mountain climb?

She was always up for a challenge. Any challenge. She was adventurous to a fault. They both were—back then. He just wished he'd been there with her at the time.

If he was, he wondered if it would have made a big difference. It seemed the Lord called her home too soon. It was way too soon for Evan.

He watched as the snow fell harder outside. Mistletoe had the most ravaging winters. But this weather also reminded him of his late wife on the mountain side. She was with other climbers at the time. None of them him.

She'd asked him to go with her, but he had business in town. Though he and his brothers lived in cabins on the massive Charming Ranch, they each had their own business endeavors. He'd spent way too much time in the office and he couldn't wait to bury himself in work.

As far as he was concerned, he didn't deserve a second chance.

"Well, we're done here," Evan said. "I'm heading back to town."

"Please tell me you're not going to the office now?" Cameron looked disappointed. "Mom's hosting the gingerbread bake-off tonight."

"I'm sorry, man. I'll call mom soon. I just need to get away from here right now."

His brother had the look on his face that he understood. Christmas time was too hard for Evan right now. He and Rhonda used to participate in all the events around this time of the year, helping out on the ranch. But not now.

He didn't know if he'd ever feel the spirit of the season again.

Was it even possible?

Chapter 2

Gwen Cameron was *not* having a good evening. She placed the chained hitch hook on the bumper of the client's car, getting ready to tow it when she heard a terrible noise coming from her own vehicle. It sounded awful. When she turned around she saw smoke coming from her own engine. Her tow truck broke down.

Oh, great.

What was she going to do now?

She was supposed to be helping a customer and now *she* needed help.

The gusty winds swirled the snow and made the visibility worse. She'd had a long day towing so many vehicles today so this was the last thing she needed.

Her father hadn't left things in a great condition. But it wasn't his fault. He'd been sick the last few months of his life.

Cameron Towing had been in her family business for decades. But after her father went to be with the lord, she was his only child, and the only one who could keep things going. There was no way she was going to let her father's business be swallowed up by the big buys.

He wanted to keep it in the family and she was going to make sure that it was kept in the family.

This wasn't exactly her line of work, though her father had showed her the ropes a few times while growing up, but she caught on quickly. Well, she caught on quickly when it came to learning new tricks of the trade, but not when it came on to knowing her best friend had helped herself to Gwen's then fiancé.

Live and learn.

She wondered if the Lord had forgotten about her. She'd hoped to be with that special someone who made her heart go pitter patter. But now the only pitter patter she heard was the sound of hale and snow on the windshield.

She turned back again to make sure her customer was all right, while she fought the bitter cold to get the broken-down vehicle secured.

Mrs. Bane was seated comfortably in the passenger side of Gwen's truck. She always made sure to take care of her clients.

Mrs. Bane was a member of the Mistletoe Church. And she had been more than caring when Gwen's dad passed away last Christmas. Mrs. Bane had brought over baked goods and soup during that time period. Always checking up on Gwen. She had told Mrs. Bane this tow was for free when she arrived on the scene. But then it looked like it wasn't even going to happen, because they were going nowhere fast.

Mrs. Bane was one of the oldest drivers in Mistletoe. At age 87, she still had remarkable energy and a quick sharp mind. Unfortunately, her little blue automobile, something she's had in her family for the longest time, wasn't as quick or sharp. And right now, Gwen was having a hard time getting it hooked up.

Gwen tried her cell phone to call for back up support from the office.

She glanced at the screen of her cell phone.

The battery was going down fast at 1%, the red bar at the top of the screen meant she needed a charger fast.

When she reached into her pockets, she realized that she didn't have her charger with her. She had a last call about an hour ago and was about to head home to recharge her phone and her own emotional battery when she got this last call from Mrs. Bane.

Mrs. Bane rolled down the window, "Are you all right, dear?" she called out.

"Mrs. Bane, I'm fine," Gwen said reassuringly. "You'd better keep the window up. It's freezing out here."

Mrs. Bane smiled and rolled the window back up.

The elder lady had been hospitalized last year for pneumonia and was prone to hypothermia as she once told the prayer group last year.

Gwen was glad to be of assistance, but it looked as if she might be running out of more than just time.

Chapter 3

Evan couldn't wait to get back to the office. There wasn't much in life he could control, such as the death of his now late wife, but there were some things he could control. His work. That's when he decided he would spend more and more time at work. Even over the holidays.

He steered his Ford Pickup down the snow-covered side road, ready to make an entrance on the main road.

The drive on the road gave him way too much time to think. He remembered when he and Rhonda drove for hours looking for the perfect Christmas tree. That was just two years ago. He had no idea that would have been the last time.

Stop that, Evan. Your brother's right. Stop obsessing over the past. It's gone. There's nothing you could ever do to bring her back.

His old man used to tell him, "You've got to live your life looking ahead not backward." And he was right.

This cowboy had to find a way to move forward, but he couldn't do it on his own.

"Oh, Lord, help me find a way to be strong again," he whispered under his breath. He used to talk to the man upstairs every day, well, his late wife used to, but those moments got less and less for him now. He knew deep down these were the times when he needed to reconnect. Right now, he needed the strength to let go of the past, the hurt, the guilt, the pain. Could he ever do that?

The silence of the night seemed to be his worst enemy right now. His thoughts raced whenever there was no noise. Maybe that's why he stayed late at the office. It was like a medication.

Being around files and reports and co-workers busying around the building.

He reached for his radio to turn it on. Maybe having sound in his truck besides the engine and the sound of his wheels grinding on the snow would be good. But the radio station played Christmas tunes 24 hours around the clock during this time of the year. His stomach lurched when he heard his late-wife's favorite Christmas song, *The First Noel.*

He loved the way his late wife had belted out the tune with her high octave vocals. It always gave him chills when she sang. His eyes stung for a moment.

He sucked in a deep breath and realized he was getting emotional. Should he switch the station? He wanted to but something urged him not to. Was it Rhonda? Was she telling him something? Was the man upstairs trying to tell him something? He wished he knew what it was.

Just then, he spotted a tow truck with blinkers on and some smoke coming from it. He saw two figures on the roadside beside a car, one of them looked like an older person. They were huddled together.

Oh, no.

His heart pumped hard and fast in his chest. He pulled over to the side, a surge of energy rushed through him.

The women looked stiff.

Was he too late?

Chapter 4

"Are you two all right?" Evan said walking closer to the two women at the side of the road.

Just then, one of them looked up. She had the most beautiful eyes he'd ever seen, but her eyes were filled with despair.

"Hi," she said, hugging the other woman.

"Hi," he said back. "What happened here?" He moved closer to them. "How can I help?"

"Thanks for offering," she said. "I'm just trying to keep her warm. Her car ended up in the snowbank there and I came to help her out."

"I see," he said, looking at the tow truck. "First let's get you two out of the cold. My pickup's nice and warm."

"Thank you. Thank you so much!" The gratitude in her voice was evident. She was humble and sweet, he could tell.

He helped the older lady up, holding on to one arm while the younger woman held onto the other.

"Oh, where am I?" the older woman said.

"Mrs. Bane, remember, your car slid into the snowbank and you called me for help."

"Oh, dear." The woman looked lost and shook her head.

Evan's heart went out to Mrs. Bane. He then realized Mrs. Bane also went to his church. She was a widow. She was married to her now late husband for over 65 years. Now, she was all alone and wanted to maintain what was left of her independence. Her life. It couldn't be easy for her. Mr. and Mrs. Bane were practically inseparable. He'd always admired that couple. He'd heard that one morning she woke up and he was gone. He went peacefully in his sleep.

Evan remembered driving his mother to the Bane's house to bring the widow some comfort and some warm pies she'd baked that day.

It was a good thing the other woman helped Mrs. Bane and got them both out of a cold vehicle.

It was dangerous, especially without some heat circulating. She did the right thing by huddling up. But what if he hadn't seen them? How long could they have kept that up? He shuddered to think about that.

This pretty lady was a tow truck operator?

He hadn't seen her before. He recognized the sign on the truck though. Maybe she was new to the company. He knew Cameron Tow Truck Service, but the old man Cam, as everyone the town called him, passed away, didn't he? Was this his daughter?

After he got the older lady in his own truck, he said, "I'm Evan Charming, by the way."

"I know," she said warmly, "I'm Gwen Cameron. Cam's daughter."

"Oh, *you're* Cam's daughter?" He eyed the beautiful woman before him with the lovely rose-colored lips and the prettiest brown eyes he'd ever seen.

Gwen.

He remembered now.

Gwen sure looked different from the last time he'd seen her. They were in elementary school and she had the biggest braids and flaming red hair. She sure looked different right now.

"I'm sorry, I didn't recognize you."

"It's okay, I've changed over the years."

Nope, she was as pretty now as she was then. Her hair looked different but that lovely oval-shaped face was still the same. He'd had a little crush on her back then. But they never kept in touch after high school. She'd moved somewhere out west. Her father carried on the shop after her mother died, so he'd heard through the small-town grapevine.

Moments later, after they'd gotten Mrs. Bane into the passenger-side seat of Evan's pickup, Gwen made some calls using Evan's cellphone since her battery died. She placed a call to Mrs. Bane's nephew to see if he could be there when they dropped Mrs. Bane home. They didn't want her to be alone on a night like tonight. She might have to see a doctor.

Right now, Evan and Gwen were on the same page. Getting Mrs. Bane to safety.

Once Mrs. Bane was inside the pickup, Evan went to survey Gwen's tow truck.

She came back to his side, her snow boots crunching in the snow.

"So, is the engine overheated?" she asked in her sweet soft voice.

He loved the sound of her voice.

Right now, this cowboy had to focus. What was he thinking? He shouldn't even be focusing on her soft sway or her lovely voice. Her tow truck and getting Gwen and Mrs. Bane to safety was the only thing on this cowboy's mind right now.

Focus, cowboy. Focus.

"It's an old engine," he said, looking under the hood. "Thankfully, it's not overheating. But you will need to get it replaced. The oil's burned."

"I see," she said, hugging herself in the chilly night.

He wished he could reach over and hug her to help her keep warm.

Evan, what's with you, man?

Stop those thoughts.

What was with him all of a sudden? Why was he having thoughts about this lovely young lady whom he went to high school with? That should be the last thing on his mind right now.

"Looks like I need to take some lessons in auto mechanic," she continued.

"It's all right. Not everyone knows that."

"I thought you were a corporate cowboy." She smiled.

"Dad taught us everything we need to know about everything," he said.

A sad feeling crept over him just now. He missed his old man. He wished his dad was still around. He always thought about his dad, especially around the holidays. His father and his mother always made it special.

He then pushed the hood of the tow truck down.

He made a call on his phone.

Later, when he'd finished he said, "I've got someone on the way with a flatbed tow. He'll be here soon to take both of your vehicles. Where can I take you ladies?"

She looked up into his eyes. For a moment, there was something there. Or maybe that was his imagination.

"Mrs. Bane's nephew said he's out of town. He can't be with her. I don't feel comfortable leaving her alone right now."

"Gotcha. I was about to say the same thing." He pulled out his cell phone again and made a call to the ranch. His mother loved Mrs. Bane and would be happy for her to stay there the night until she was all right.

"Okay, it's settled," he said.

"What is?"

"My mother would be happy to stay with Mrs. Bane, either at her home or at the ranch."

Gwen's appreciative smile was infectious. Her eyes lit up when she knew Mrs. Bane would be all right.

Just then a thought struck him. Wasn't Mrs. Bane on the Women's Ministry with his mother? She was one of church's matchmakers, wasn't she?

Oh, boy. Talk about timing.

His mother had been on him to find a match and said the Lord worked in mysterious ways.

He immediately swept the thought out of his mind. That was the last thing he wanted to be thinking about. He wished he could turn off his heart's feelings. He was sure it was nothing. He didn't celebrate Christmas and he didn't believe in love again. Not anymore. His ship had sailed when his wife passed.

"How does that sound to you, Mrs. Bane?" Evan said to the older woman as she leaned back comfortably in the passenger side seat. "Do you want to visit the Charming Ranch? Or would you like my mother to drop by and stay with you for a while."

Mrs. Bane's eyes lit up; her smile wide. "Yes, dear. I would love that. If it's no trouble. I don't want to pull her away from her family."

"Oh, it's no trouble at all, Ma'am. She would love to visit you."

"Thank you for doing that?" Gwen said to Evan. "I really appreciate it."

"Hey, like I said. It's no trouble at all."

He liked that Gwen treated Mrs. Bane as if she were her own grandmother. Gwen had always had a heart of gold from what he remembered about her in high school. She used to rescue all the little stray pets in the town. He was surprised she didn't go into veterinarian medicine instead of her father's business.

"Well, let's get going. I'll pick up my mother and then we'll head out to Mrs. Bane's house. The flatbed's on its way to your truck."

"Thanks so much again."

Moments later, just as Evan was about to join the ladies in his truck, his cell phone buzzed again as he stood outside his pickup.

He looked at the screen.

His face fell.

It was bad news.

Chapter 5

Well, this charming handsome cowboy knew everything.

A warm glow came over Gwen when she'd watched Evan earlier as he assessed her truck after making sure she and Mrs. Bane were all right.

She snuggled into the seat beside Mrs. Bane. Evan's pickup truck was spacious and very comfy. It had three spacious seats in the back as well as up front.

What would she have done if the Lord hadn't sent this cowboy at the right time? She didn't want to think about it. Her mind came up with all sorts of horrible scenarios of what could have happened.

But he came right in the nick of time. And to that, she would be forever grateful.

Gwen admired that about Evan. Stepping up the plate. Pulling over to help a person out.

Finally, she got a chance to meet up with him again.

She wondered if he even remembered her from high school. Did he? Well, she sure remembered him. But he was off limits then. A Charming brother. And they were off limits to most of the girls in the school. For one thing, he was a senior when she was a junior. Secondly, only the popular girls in school had a chance with him.

Evan was different from all the other guys. She remembered that. He was different from the other Charming brothers, who by the way, all lived up to their name. They were sweet, charismatic cowboys who worked hard and played even harder.

They all left the ranch after high school to pursue college careers as far as she remembered. Evan set up his own ad agency and worked on spreading the message about agriculture. He worked mostly with agricultural clients since he knew so much about the industry, growing up on one of the largest ranches in the district.

A tall, dark and handsome cowboy on a cold and chilly night.

Speaking of which, after she made sure Mrs. Bane was cozy in the passenger seat, she turned her head to look outside to see Evan.

The look on his face concerned her.

Why were his brows furrowed all of a sudden?

"Everything all right?" she asked after he ended his call and got back into the truck.

"I'm afraid not. Looks like the roads are blocked back into town," he said. "A fallen tree."

"Oh, no."

"There's no way we could get Mrs. Bane to the ranch now. We have a lot of rooms at the main house but I don't think we could get there safely," he assessed with a take-charge tone in his voice.

"Are you sure?" Gwen asked.

"Going west is our best bet, right now."

The heavy gusts of winds swept snow all around the truck. The sharp chilly feel of snow pellets had hit her face earlier when she was outside.

She couldn't wait to get home.

Evan excused himself and made another phone call. Probably to let his mother know they wouldn't be back to the ranch.

Gwen remembered he got married a few years back. But then she'd heard his wife died on a mountain climb. How terrible! Her heart went out to him. She heard it was around the holiday time too, if she was not mistaken.

"And?" she asked, curiously.

"Well, the main house is out of reach right now. Tree fell there too."

"We can take Mrs. Bane home, but we have to figure out how to get around the blockage."

"You can stay at my place until the storm blows over," Mrs. Bane said. "I insist. Besides, I don't feel too good being on my own right now. Why don't you two stay for a while."

"That's awfully nice of you, Mrs. Bane. But are you sure?" Evan asked.

"I'm very sure. It would mean a lot to me."

Evan glanced at the screen of his phone.

"We'll be happy to help you out Mrs. Bane and we appreciate the offer of staying for a while. Storm's getting worse right now. The Town just tweeted for everyone to stay indoors."

"Then that settles it," Mrs. Bane said. "Let's stay indoors, at my cabin."

Stay indoors?

Oh, no. Would Mrs. Bane be okay with having visitors in her home tonight? Would she be okay with that?

Could Gwen stay in a small cabin with a cowboy on this stormy night?

Chapter 6

Evan drove off the main road to the back street, hoping to find a way to get safely to Mrs. Bane's cabin on the west side. He'd been there before. The gusts of wind and snow pellets pounded the windshield. His visibility decreased by the moment on this dark snowy night, but he was determined. He prayed to the man upstairs to get them safely to Mrs. Bane's house. Right now, he thought he needed a miracle.

"You ladies all right?" he asked, not taking his eyes off the road blanketed in heavy thick snow. The tires grinded on the crunchy snow.

The ladies nodded and said they were good.

He was careful not to push on the gas too much. He would get there safely.

"You mind if we play some music?" Gwen asked.

"Go right ahead."

"Thanks." Her phone was already charging in his car. She turned on her music on her iPhone. It played some sweet Christmas songs.

He wished he could feel that Christmas spirit, but it was no use. Maybe he should have told her he'd choose the song selection and choose something not so festive.

Mrs. Bane's head rested on the headrest. She looked like she was half asleep.

The scent of Gwen's perfume wafted to his nose. She smelled delicious. What was that fragrance?

His heart reacted to the way her hand brushed his arm as she swiped to get the songs she wanted to play on her phone.

He sucked in a deep breath.

Focus, cowboy.

You shouldn't be feeling anything for Gwen.

"What's your favorite Christmas song?" she asked.

"The First Noel," he said. "What's yours?"

She looked startled.

"What's wrong?"

She grinned. "Nothing. That's my favorite one too. Especially the melody."

"Me too," he said, surprised.

"What's your favorite Christmas memory?" she asked him, probably trying to pass the time as they made their way through the dark snowy night.

"I don't have one."

Now he wasn't being honest, was he?

"Everyone has one."

"I don't. Not anymore."

"But you *do* celebrate it."

"I acknowledge it, of course. But all the parties and get-togethers...Just not for me."

"I'm sorry to hear that. Hope you change your mind later."

"Why?"

"It's such a magical time of the year. Such a special time. There's nothing like the spirit of the season."

"I'm sure. But I just don't feel it. Don't think I ever will."

"What happened to you to make you feel that way?" she probed as if she wanted to fix it.

"I'd rather not get into it, right now."

"I understand." She looked out the window. He could swear he saw the look of hurt in her pretty eyes.

Oh, no. He hoped and prayed he didn't hurt her feelings. That was not his intention. But he didn't want to get into the fact that his wife died over the Christmas holidays and he wasn't even by her side.

He also hoped the drive to Mrs. Bane's cabin would be shorter. He couldn't take all this tension. It wasn't her fault he was grumpy about celebrating the holidays. The lovely lady had a good spirit about her. He just didn't think he deserved to have any of it.

"So," he said to break the silence. "What's *your* favorite holiday memory?" he asked Gwen while Mrs. Bane slept like a baby.

"Family gatherings, church nativity plays. It's always fun. Well, it was when dad was around."

"I'm really sorry for your loss. Cam was a good man."

"Thank you. He passed around the holidays last year."

"Man, I'm really sorry about that."

"It's okay." She waited for him to say something else. He could sense that. But he wasn't' ready to talk about his late wife.

He's sure Gwen must have heard about the accident on the mountain. The whole town heard. But then again, maybe Gwen was out of town at the time.

Later, on the drive, Mrs. Bane woke up. She and Gwen started singing Christmas carols as they drove through the snow-covered roads towards Mrs. Bane's cabin.

Evan wanted to feel the spirit. But he just couldn't. Guilt prevented him from doing that. Still, the lovely lips and breathtaking smile on Gwen's face and they she lit up as they sang, made him feel something inside. But he had to push those feelings away.

Finally, they made it to the Bane's cabin. The driveway was filled with about a foot of snow.

Evan got out of the truck and grabbed his shovel in the back. Then he began shovelling.

"Oh, dear. The snow is so high," Mrs. Bane said as Gwen helped her out of the truck. "I didn't get to put salt on the driveway."

"No problem, Mrs. Bane," Evan said.

"Please be careful."

"I will, Ma'am." Evan shovelled a pathway first to get Mrs. Bane safely inside. After Gwen helped Mrs. Bane up the walkway to her home, Evan continued to shovel the driveway.

"Please be careful," Mrs. Bane said again, this time from the top of her steps as she stood by the door to go inside. "It's slippery."

"I will..." Evan said again, this time, his boots went up as he slipped on the driveway.

Evan shook his head and grinned, trying to ignore the sharp pain in his side.

Great. This was really great.

"Oh, no. Are you all right?" Gwen called out from the top of the steps after Mrs. Bane was safely inside.

"Just thought I'd look up at the stars while laying on my back," he teased.

Gwen burst out laughing and came down to help him.

He propped himself to sit up.

He just wanted to sit there for a second. As he sat up on the driveway, he heard steps beside him crunching in the snow. It was Gwen standing there with her hand help out for him to get up.

She certainly was quite a girl.

He could get up on his own, of course. But he held out his gloved hand. And she took his. He stood up. There was a nice feeling holding her hand. He tried to tell her to stand still, but it was too late, she moved one boot and she went down too.

"Are you all right?" he asked, trying to catch her fall—but they both landed down on the slippery ground.

She burst out laughing as the wind blew snow around them.

"Well, isn't this something," she said.

He actually liked the feeling of holding her in his arms. There was something that felt comfortable about Gwen. A strange yet delightful feeling swirled around him. What was that feeling? He wasn't supposed to be feeling anything this year. Nothing at all.

Just then, after they'd both propped themselves back up on the driveway, holding each other, she bent down to scoop up a ball of fresh snow in her hands.

Oh, no.

She hurled a snowball towards him.

He scooped up snow as well. "So this is how it's going down, huh?" he asked, jokingly.

She placed her hands on her hips. Then she bent down on grabbed some more snow.

"Thanks for the fall," she joked, and hurled snow at him.

He did the same and scooped up some snow and gently tossed it in her direction.

"That's all you've got?" she laughed, hands on her hips.

"Didn't want to hurt you. You know, you being a girl and all."

"Oh, really now? You think I'm fragile, do you?" She grabbed an even larger ball of snow.

Before long they were laughing and engaged in a lovely snowball fight.

He couldn't' remember the last time he had so much fun.

A light energy came over him.

It was as if his late wife was telling him, it's okay. It's okay to move forward and get on with your life. It was as if she was up in heaven looking down on him, giving him her approval. Letting him know she was all right where she was.

Lightness came over his heart. Would this last?

***

"What's this?" Evan said later inside the cabin. Earlier, they'd finished up their snowball fight and cleaned up the driveway so the snow wouldn't accumulate too much by the morning.

He was stunned to see the place so beautifully decorated. He didn't want to be reminded of Christmas again. He already did his part to decorate the ranch. But this little cozy cottage was a winter wonderland.

"You like?" Gwen said, cheerfully, taking off her jacket and hat and scarf and gloves and placing them by the side on the coat rack. "I helped Mrs. Bane decorate her cottage for the holiday the other day."

"You did all this?" He was surprised. He didn't think the cute tow truck driver had time to pretty up someone's cottage. Christmas and the winter season were the busiest times of the year in Mistletoe for the tow truck industry.

"Sure did." She paused for a moment as if studying his face. "You're not too happy." It sounded more like a statement than a question.

"Oh, no. I just…It's okay."

She wanted to say something else, but…she didn't.

"I had fun out there tonight," Gwen said. "Never thought I'd have a belly laugh like that in a long while. Not after, well…my dad passed…."

"Of course. It must be hard."

"Some days are better than others. He was always into the Christmas spirit and his laugh was infectious," she said.

Just like yours, he wanted to say.

Just then Mrs. Bane came out with a tray of hot chocolate and freshly baked biscuits.

"When did you make these? I thought you were asleep," Gwen said, surprised.

"Oh, I wanted to make you both something for being so kind staying here with me until the storm settles down to make sure I'm all right. And you must be cold after shovelling my driveway."

"It was no problem, Mrs. Bane," Evan said.

"Yes, it was no problem at all."

"Here you go," she said, placing the tray down.

"Thank you so much," they both said in unison.

Mrs. Bane had a wide grin on her lips. And Evan thought he saw a wink in her left eye. Or was that his imagination?

"Aren't you having any?" Evan asked as he helped Mrs. Bane take the mugs off the tray and onto the table.

"Oh, I'm fine," she said. "You two enjoy your hot chocolate and biscuits. Let me know if you need anything else. I'm going upstairs to rest a little."

"Of course, no trouble."

The trays had lovely gingerbread cookies laid out beautifully just as his mother used to make. The hot chocolates had a candy cane inside each cup, topped with fresh whipped cream.

"That's awfully kind of you, Mrs. Bane."

"Think nothing of it. See you both later." She made her way upstairs as Evan and Gwen sat down in the living room.

Oh, boy.

If he didn't know any better, he'd swear Mrs. Bane had something up her sleeve. He was willing to bet she was about to call his mother.

Now, what was he going to talk to Gwen about?

Chapter 7

There was an awkward silence between Evan and Gwen for a moment after Mrs. Bane left them alone in the living room.

"Lovely tree," he commented.

"Thanks. It's not finished. Would you like to help me finish decorating it?"

She walked over to the corner to pick up a large box of ornaments.

"Here, let me help you with that," he said.

He placed his cup down on the table and walked over to where she was. He scooped up the heavy box and their hands brushed for the first time without gloves. He felt a tingle inside.

"Sorry," she said.

"For what?"

"Oh, nothing."

A moment lingered between them. Evan couldn't help but notice she had the prettiest blue eyes he'd ever seen. Her eyes were blue as a cloudless sky on a warm summer day.

"These are nice," he said, after he placed the box down beside the tree and opened it.

"I got some of the items from the market. And some of them are from Mrs. Bane's old house in the attic. They mean a lot to her."

"It's very nice of you to help her out."

"It's nothing. Mrs. Bane was also a friend of my dad. And I miss my Grandma who passed away when I was much younger. Mrs. Bane became another grandma to me in a way."

His heart melted at her warmth and her sentimentality.

"You're good with taking care of people," he commented, wanting to know more about the girl he hardly knew in high school. The girl who always mesmerized him from afar.

"Thanks. I took care of my dad last year when..."

"I know it must be difficult," he said, his voice soft and low.

"Yes, it was."

Her eyes misted.

He wanted to hug her, to comfort her.

But she wiped her eyes and started to place another ornament on the tree.

"I was out of town on business when it happened. When he got the call from the doctor," she said, fixing up one of the branches on the tree. "So, I left my job and came back here to take care of him. To be with him."

"That was very nice of you."

He'd never met a girl like that who'd sacrifice so much. Just give up everything to help a loved one. A parent.

Then again, if he were in her shoes, he'd probably do the same thing.

"My father gave so much to the family. He always took care of us. It was the least I could do. I didn't want him to be all alone." Her tone sounded stronger.

She tried to put up a brave front but he could tell in her eyes, she was still hurting. He knew a thing or two about the pain of losing someone close to you.

She looked stunning against the backdrop of the beautifully lit Christmas tree with the lovely flickering lights, like a million tiny lightbulbs.

"So that's why you took over the tow-truck business?"

"I had no choice. Dad made it clear when he knew he didn't have much time that he didn't want the Altons to buy him out."

"The Altons?" Evan was stunned. "What do they have to do with this?"

His family knew the Altons very well. They were considered loan sharks and they sometimes went under another name as alternate lenders. They were more like dangerous lenders.

They weren't the nicest people in town. In fact, he'd had some run-ins with them before when they tried to blackmail his now late father. They gave his old man a lot of stress. He had to have a few words with them about that. And it wasn't pretty. They backed off eventually. But he hoped no one else he knew would get involved with them, if he could help it.

"My dad borrowed money from them when things were slow during the recession."

"I see." Evan clenched his jaw.

"He regretted every moment he owed them," she continued. "The interest rates were out of this world. He ended up owing more than double the amount he borrowed. I wished I'd known then. But my dad was so proud that he didn't tell anyone else about it at the time."

"So what happened to the loan?"

"He couldn't pay it off. And I had helped him with his medical bills..."

Evan's heart squeezed in his chest. He really felt her pain. He wanted to comfort her, to hold her, to let her know she'd done good by her dad and that he wanted to help her the rest of the way. He listened attentively, admiring her, wanting to be there for her.

He didn't know why this feeling came over him. Ever since his wife passed, he wanted nothing to do with anyone, especially women. He just wanted to close himself off from the world. But Gwen was a different story. All of a sudden, he wanted to be in her world.

Why was he feeling this way?

He couldn't save his now late wife, but maybe he could save Gwen—in a different way.

He told everyone he no longer felt the Christmas spirit, but he was beginning to rethink that.

"So," she continued "I gave up my condo and my job and contacted my dad's loyal customers and let them know I would be taking over. They were relieved to hear that. No one wanted to deal with the Altons."

"I don't blame them," he added.

He wanted to know if there was someone in her life who was there for her at the time.

But she answered his question as if she could hear this thoughts.

"My ex had left me at the time."

"I'm sorry to hear that."

"No, I'm not. It was for the best. He couldn't handle a woman doing a so-called man's job."

"That's too bad for him. His loss. You don't need a guy like that."

"Thank you. He also left with some of my savings. But that's okay. You live and you learn."

"What did he do?" Fury surged through Evan. He disliked when a man took advantage of a woman's kindness. It robbed him the wrong way.

"Some scheme, he wanted me to invest in. Like I said, I'm not bothered by it now. Things can turnaround anytime. Just got to have a little faith and put in a little work."

"True." He agreed.

She grinned. "Unfortunately, we didn't have many funds to get a new fleet of tow trucks and as you found out, the one I'm driving is pretty old, in bad shape."

"Listen, don't worry about that. I've got you covered."

"You? Oh, no." She shook her head. "I can't do that. You've done enough already."

"Seriously, it's no big deal. My friend's working on your truck now. Please don't worry about the charge. Besides, I owe your old man one." A smile touched his lips. "He'd helped me out on quite a few tows during the day. Especially when I got my first car." He chuckled.

She grinned. "Your first car? That was you?" She placed her hands on her hips. "Did you happen to drive an old Sunfire back in the day?"

He smiled. "That thing got me from point A to B."

"And C," she added. "Dad told me about a young guy with a Sunfire that had its days in the sun."

"Yeah. In the sun and in the ditch. A long time ago."

They both grinned and looked into each other's eyes. They locked gaze for a moment and he felt his heart beat faster.

"So...what about you?" she said, as she placed more ornaments on the Christmas tree.

He noticed a hint of rouge on her lovely cheeks.

"You don't work on the ranch, do you?" she said. "I haven't seen you around."

"I do. Sometimes I help out. I grew up on the ranch. But right now, I have my own business, spreading awareness about agriculture and helping other businesses."

"Advertising. That's right. I heard that one of the Charmings had an ad agency. That's sweet. Must be a lot of fun putting those campaigns together."

He paused for a moment. Was it fun? In the beginning it was. But now it was a place to bury his head, not wanting to deal with the reality that his beloved wife was gone.

And speaking of which, he was supposed to be in the office working on a campaign for the new year for one of his clients. He didn't like the fact that he was going to be spending the holidays in his office building instead of on the ranch with his family.

Guilt swept over him. His mother wanted him to be there for the Christmas Barn Hall Dance and he'd told her he'd be working. He didn't want to show up alone. He didn't want to enjoy the celebration.

"It was a lot of fun, until..." His voice broke off.

"Are you all right?" Her voice was soft.

"My wife passed last year, around the holidays."

"Oh, Evan. I'm so sorry for your loss." Her genuine expression of sorrow gave him some comfort.

"I know what it's like to lose a loved one over the holidays," she added. "I know it can't be easy. I can't imagine a spouse."

"Thank you," he said softly.

"Your wife is with the Lord know. Just my like Dad."

Just then, he felt comfort wrap around him.

"Yes, they are," he agreed.

He knew he should have felt some comfort before. But he refused to feel anything but anger at the time, but as the year passed, he'd gotten used to the fact that his beloved wife was not coming back. But she was up in heaven now. He had to find some way to move forward. But it was hard. Guilt was a hard pill to swallow.

"Are you going to be all right?" she asked.

"I felt like it was my fault she's not here now."

Her face looked alarmed. "Why do you say that?"

"She was on a mountain climbing trip. And I was busy working at the office on a campaign and I didn't want to go with her..."

"Oh, no. I'm so sorry to hear that. But Evan, you have to know it's not your fault."

"Isn't it?" he said, but instantly felt regret that he snapped at his new friend.

"No. It isn't. Do you know why?"

"Why?"

"Because you cannot predict the future. None of us can. You had no idea what was going to happen. I heard about that accident on the mountain side. It was terrible. I don't know what I could say to let you know that you couldn't have known."

"You're right, but I feel as if..."

"As if what?" she asked gently. And he instantly felt soothed by her lovely warm tone as warm as honey.

"Maybe I don't want to feel happy."

"I think your late wife would have wanted you to be okay."

It was as if his wife was around them, her spirit anyway. And it was as if she was telling Evan it's all right.

"She loved mountain climbing right? Her name was Rhonda, right?"

"Yes."

She sucked in a deep breath. "I can't believe it's the same lady. Do you know something?"

"What is it?"

"I actually towed her car once.'

"That was you? I was out of town on business once, when she told me her car broke down, but the tow person was kind and gave her a ride to finish her shopping."

He felt warm that this tow truck lady was so kind and caring.

"Yes, I'd taken over my dad's business while he was sick the last two years of his life. And I got a chance to meet your late wife. She was lovely. And do you know what she told me."

"What did she tell you?"

"That life's an adventure. She loved living it."

His heart exploded with emotion in his chest.

It was as if Rhonda was speaking through Gwen.

"Yes, she always said that," he commented with a smile.

"That means you should have comfort in knowing that she lived her life the way she wanted to. And she left here doing something she lived for..."

She was right.

It was as if the Lord brought Gwen into his life right now for a reason.

"You know something, I've never thought about it that way after that...incident."

She touched his arm and he felt a wave of emotion. A good emotion. The spirit of the season. It was as if his guilt had washed away. But he wanted to do more for Gwen now. She had no idea what she'd just done for him.

"I wish I could do something special for you."

"I think you already have."

Here was this beautiful tow truck driver with a heart of gold and warmth and love and insight. He wanted to see her again.

But maybe he should ask her to the barn dance. No, it's probably a bad idea to even think of asking Gwen. Or maybe it wasn't.

"Gwen, would you like to come with me to the Christmas Barn Hall Dance?"

She took a deep breath. "I'm sorry. I...I can't."

She looked very sorry she had to turn him down.

His heart sank.

"No problem," he said casually, trying to brush off it. "Just thought I'd ask."

Was he ever going to see Gwen again?

Chapter 8

After the snowstorm settled and Mrs. Bane was comfortable, Evan checked around the house with Gwen to make sure everything was safe.

"Okay, looks like we're done here." He and Gwen told Mrs. Bane goodbye and to call them if she needed anything.

Gwen appreciated this cowboy's take charge and caring demeanor. She also appreciated him spending extra time with her and Mrs. Bane. And for taking care of her tow truck.

"You are really amazing, you know that cowboy," Gwen said to Evan after they sat in his truck.

"I am?"

"Yes, you did a lot tonight helping us out and then staying with us long after the storm settled down."

"Hey, it was nothing. Anytime."

"Do you mean that?"

"I wouldn't say it if I didn't," the cowboy grinned and she saw the lovely smile on his lips.

Those lips of his.

She was embarrassed to admit, she wondered what they would feel like on hers.

Okay, calm down now Gwen. He's probably unavailable. Emotionally.

He was a widower, after all. And who could blame him for taking his time?

He had, however, invited her to the barn dance.

She told him she couldn't go. Why did she say that?

Was she afraid of dating again?

She wished she could go. She really liked him. A lot. But she had work to do. Christmas holidays was her company's busiest season. There was no way she could slack off now.

"So, where to?" he asked.

She gave him her address.

"Are you sure, you'll be all right tonight?" Evan asked Gwen later when they arrived at her home. The home she grew up in. The home her father spent his last days.

She noticed Evan's eyebrows furrowed with concern.

Was he worried about her? That was so sweet of him.

She sighed deeply.

"Yes. I will be fine," she said.

Though deep down, she wished they could chat over a cup of coffee. Just like they'd done over at Mrs. Bane's house. But it was getting late. And she had to be up early to check on what's happening with her tow truck. And he probably had work to do to. He'd told her that he had been on his way to his office when he saw her stranded on the roadside with Mrs. Bane.

Was he going to go back to the office now?

"That's the house I grew up in," she said. "I'll make sure everything's locked up."

"I can come and look around the house first, if you like?"

"That's so sweet of you. I'm fine. Really."

"Okay, but I'll be waiting out here until you give me the signal you're good. Deal?"

She grinned. Was he charming or what?

"Deal?"

Gwen walked into the home and turned on her lights, while Evan waited outside his truck. Ready to come in if she needed him.

When she turned on the lights. She screamed.

Chapter 9

"What the...?"

The scream coming from Gwen's house caused Evan to rush from his truck towards the direction of the sound.

"Are you all right?" he asked once he got inside the front door and held her.

She then shook her head and grinned. "I'm sorry, Evan."

Evan's eyes followed her gaze.

A man sat in the corner of the living room. He looked as if he hadn't shaved in years.

"Who are you?" Evan asked, firmly. "What are you doing here?"

"I'm just here to see my little sister," he said, his hands up in the air as if he was surrendering.

"Is this man your brother?" Evan asked, surprised. He didn't realize old man Cam had more than one child. He thought he didn't have a son.

"Yes, he's my half-brother. My mother had a child before she met my father. My brother and I just got to know each other a few years back."

He surveyed Gwen's face to make sure she was okay.

"I'm really sorry to scare you sis, really." The man looked apologetic.

The man seemed harmless enough and very sorry. And very frail.

"No worries. What are you doing in town?" She then asked. "I'm glad to see you but with you breaking into my home and surprising me like this..."

"Man, I'm so sorry. I wanted to surprise you, not scare you. And I didn't break in. The back door was open."

She gave him a really-now look.

"Is that true?" Evan asked, wanting nothing more than to protect her.

"Yes. Sometimes I leave the back door open..."

Evan politely interjected. "I wish you wouldn't do that. It's not safe. It's a small town and everybody knows everybody, but you never know...There are a lot of visitors coming in and out of town every day."

"True," she agreed. "Listen, I'm fine. You can leave. I know you must have a lot of work to do."

"Just as long as you're fine."

"I am."

Just then the image of his wife, flashed in his mind.

Gwen smiled with appreciation. "That's very sweet of you to offer, but we're good."

***

"You like him, don't you?" her brother Rex said later.

"He's a nice cowboy." Gwen smiled.

"And you like him."

"I like him as a friend."

"Oh, come on. I can tell the way you two look at each other. You both look like you're connected."

"Connected?" she asked, making a fresh pot of tea.

"Yes."

"Okay, don't change the subject. What are you doing here? And why did you break into my house?"

"Babs left me."

"Oh, no. I'm so sorry to hear that."

"Well, actually, she kicked me out. I need a place to stay."

"You can stay here as long as you like."

"Thanks, sis."

She poured their cups with steaming hot tea. Perfect for a wintery night like tonight. It was a good thing Evan was around at the time though. What if it *had* been an intruder. She shuddered to think about that.

"What's on your mind, sis? You're in a daze."

"I am not."

"When are you two going out?"

"We're not."

"And why not? He seems like a nice guy. A lot nicer than that rat you dated a few years back when I first met you."

"Yes, Evan is so much nicer. But..."

"But what?"

"I'm not ready to date again. I've got to focus on keeping Dad's business afloat."

"That doesn't mean you can't share your journey with someone. I just felt something there between you two. I like the way he was going to throw me out on my behind if I was an intruder."

Gwen smiled.

"I mean, I wouldn't have liked it, but I like that he's looking out for my little sis."

She did appreciate Evan's protectiveness and his support. But she didn't want to get too close to another man again. Her heart was still healing after her ex. She really should focus on her business.

But what if she missed her chance at happiness again?

Was it too late?

Evan would probably meet someone else at his family's Christmas barn dance. It was too late. She'd already told the cowboy, no.

She was never going to see him again.

Chapter 10

"So, you decided to show up this year?" Evan's brother Cameron said to him the following week at the Charming Ranch Annual Christmas Barn Hall Dance.

He missed last year, after Rhonda passed. And he'd vowed to never attend again. But here he was.

Holiday music was sounding through the speakers and guests were filing in. At least he made it, but he didn't feel as if he were there spiritually. Just physically. Maybe it would take some time to get into the groove of things again.

His thoughts were also on Gwen. Maybe she was busy with the tow service. She had business to tend to, after all.

Last week, he'd made sure that she got her truck in pristine condition. She was very thankful. But then he hadn't seen her since. He'd been back at the office working on his latest client's proposal for a new year campaign. And all that time, his mind was on Gwen.

"What's wrong?" Cameron asked.

Evan couldn't help the feeling of sadness that washed over him. The truth was, he missed Gwen's company. That day in the snow and while they were helping Mrs. Bane meant a lot to him. He hadn't smiled or connected with anyone in a long while and he knew now that he'd been missing something. He had so much fun that day—and he could tell that she did too. He'd thought the Lord brought two lost souls who'd lost loved ones together for a reason. But maybe it wasn't meant to last. Just a flash in the pan.

If he were being honest with himself, he would love to see Gwen again.

He would love to have that kiss under the mistletoe.

The magic of the Charming Ranch mistletoe kiss was that those who kissed under it would be blessed with a long and happy relationship.

Yes, it was true that ancient cultures revered the mistletoe for its healing properties and it was always a sign of good luck to those who kissed under it.

Last week, Evan had offered to have someone fill in for Gwen so she could have some fun and come to the barn hall dance.

Everyone in the community who attended always had a blast. She'd told him she would love to go to the dance but was afraid of business slipping during a busy time, so she had to decline his offer.

No problem, he thought. But there was a problem. He was missing her like crazy. And he wanted her to relax at least one day during the holiday season. She seemed to be working overtime everyday catching up on work. She was a trooper. And he admired that about her.

"Darling son, I'm so glad you came," his mother said.

"I'm happy to be here."

"You never know, you might find that special someone to kiss under the mistletoe this year."

His mother always tried to play matchmaker for her sons. Just then he saw Mrs. Bane.

"Well, Mrs. Bane, how are you doing?" he asked.

"Never better. Thank you again for rescuing me last week."

"Oh, it was my pleasure."

"Oh, no. It was *my* pleasure. I love bringing people together." She winked.

He had no idea why Mrs. Bane winked just now. Only that she was a sly little matchmaker.

The party was a success. But it was getting late. And Evan wanted to return to his office.

When Evan turned around to leave. His jaw fell open.

There she was. A stunning beauty.

Wow!

Gwen strolled through the door like a princess. Her lovely mane of hair swept up in a gracious style. Her face pretty as a princess. Her gown hugged her body, showing off her lovely curves.

He was stunned into silence.

"You came," he said, walking closer to her.

"I thought about what you said. And well, I took up your offer. Your friend is covering for me. I can't thank you enough."

"Hey, it's my pleasure. I'm glad you're here."

"Me too,."

"You look *beautiful*. Amazing," he complimented.

"Thank you. So do you," she gushed. "I mean, handsome. You look handsome in your suit."

He thanked her for her compliment.

Moments later, Evan saw Mrs. Bane and his mother eyeing him and Gwen lovingly as the couple danced.

He couldn't help but grin.

He loved the scent of Gwen's perfume. Her smooth skin touched his as they slow danced.

He just realized as Mrs. Bane and his mother talked in a corner looking over at them, grinning, that Mrs. Bane probably wanted them to talk that night she asked both of them to stay in her living room over a cup of hot chocolate.

A warm smile curved his lips.

"This is wonderful," Gwen said. "I hope we can see each other after this."

"I would like that," he said.

She looked up and smiled.

"Isn't that the famous mistletoe?"

He too looked up. "It sure is."

"How about it, cowboy?"

She leaned up to him and he leaned down.

He could not believe this was happening.

He brushed his lips over hers and they shared the most memorable kiss ever. He tingled inside after their kiss.

It was magical.

Special.

A true blessing to be given a second chance.

Evan believed in the magic of Christmas again. The Christmas spirit came over him once more. He looked forward to spending more time with Gwen. He knew one thing for sure, he was never going to stop counting his blessings.

***

Thank you for reading *Cowboy's Christmas Blessing (Rescued by the Cowboy at Christmas Book 2)*.

Bonus excerpt of "Cowboy Under the Mistletoe" is on the next page...

Cowboy Under the Mistletoe

A cowboy with a broken heart. An ex-fiancée with a secret...

Carter Charming stopped celebrating the holidays after his fiancée, Paige, left him without a word. So he swore he'd never marry, never date, and he avoided mistletoes like it was going out of style. But when the magic of Christmas flows over the small town of Mistletoe and his mother plays a little matchmaking, will this stubborn cowboy change his mind?

Chapter 1

A wave of anxiety swept through Paige Louisa as the snow flurries fell harder on her windshield. Her pulse pounded hard inside her chest.

Charlie.

I have to find Charlie.

Where is he?

Why did he run off like that?

Oh, Lord please keep him safe out there.

He had to be somewhere around the area. Where could he be right now? Why did this have to happen?

Paige's visibility tapered off by the minute as she drove slowly down the road passing colorful bright lights and Christmas decorations on this dark winter night. She was feeling anything but festive right now.

The town of Mistletoe was known for its brutal winter storms. And she just had to be visiting now.

He couldn't have gotten far, could he? Her friend Daphne was in tears when she told Paige that Charlie had ran off. Paige had left Charlie at her friend's house while she went into town.

She prayed to God to help her find him before anything happened to him.

Paige was beginning to wonder if coming back to Mistletoe was a mistake.

She agreed to come back to town to help out with the Annual Christmas sleigh ride for the kids at the hospital.

After her father passed recently, she thought it would be a good idea. Especially since Christmas would be in four weeks.

She didn't want to be alone. This was also the time of the year her mother passed, two years ago. And now her father passed before Christmas. She believed her dad died of a broken heart. His wife and best friend of 40 years was gone. Seeing her die slowly had crushed his soul and his spirit. Paige had left Mistletoe to go back to her home city in Texas to spend time with him to help him to heal.

She'd left Mistletoe at that time. And she had to break up with her now former fiancé without so much as a word. Even though it tore her up inside to do that, she felt she had no other choice. She never did get to explain why.

If he found out about her, he probably wouldn't want anything to do with her. So it was for the best.

Still, memories of spending Christmas with her ex-fiancé Carter and his family flooded her mind with a warm feeling.

His family really knew how to celebrate the holidays. They always went all out with the best decorations; brightest lights and they even hosted the Annual sleigh ride with the huskies. Her stomach knotted with anxiety thinking she might see him again. But she couldn't think about that right now. She hadn't even planned to step foot back in Mistletoe until now.

Daphne also encouraged her to come back to Mistletoe for the lighting of the town Christmas Tree, the most beautiful tree in the county. The mayor had also invited her to come too. She'd designed the new Children's Play Center at the Mistletoe Children's Hospital. She was an interior designer and submitted her entry during a contest. She always loved making things beautiful. Too bad those skills didn't translate to her love life.

Her design had won a prestigious award and she'd become a bit of a local celebrity for her innovative approach to making a place calm, entertaining and relaxing at the same time. Her Instagram page had hundreds of thousands of likes. But what her followers didn't know was that she was anything but happy.

She'd moved from small town Mistletoe to her home city be closer to her mother when she became ill. And then she stayed to take care of her father. But while she was there she'd facetimed her then fiancé and told him she couldn't go through with the wedding. She thought she could let him down easy. But there was nothing easy about breaking up with the man who was supposed to be the love of your life. Carter Charming, a tall and handsome cowboy who lived up to his last name.

Carter was Mistletoe's beloved cowboy running the famous Charming Ranch, a ranch resort in the small town of Mistletoe. She knew she'd become an enemy of the town for breaking his heart. Small town close-knit community meant everybody knew everybody's business. And she couldn't even tell him the real reason why she left him—she couldn't tell *anyone*.

He'd leave you anyway if he really found out about you.

She found out something about herself when she went back home. It was something she couldn't share with Carter.

Just then as Paige's car hit a bump in the road. She swerved over to the side; her tires slid into the ditch.

Oh, no.

She was stuck.

There was practically zero visibility with the snowfall. She was practically in the middle of nowhere.

Would anyone find her in time?

If she stepped out of her car, she might freeze to death, but if she stayed inside, she wouldn't be any better off, would she?

She'd heard about what happened to that couple who stayed in their car and froze. But then again, was it because they didn't turn on the heat for five minutes every hour?

Numbness filled Paige's body.

How would she find Charlie now?

What if she died? What if this was it?

What was she going to do now?

She prayed to the Lord to protect her, to show her a way out. But she had a sinking feeling it might be too late?

***

Carter Charming paused and watched as the pretty snowflakes fell hard over Charming Ranch, his family's ranch in Mistletoe. He then went back to his task, fixing the Christmas lights on the barn.

Sadness swept over him when he thought about how much he missed his dear dad. His father and he used to put up the lights on the barn at this time of the year. His father made living on the ranch a lot of fun for his sons.

It had been one year now since his old man's passing. And he missed him like crazy. Christmas at Charming Ranch Resort was a magical time of the year for the town. They went all out and decorated the land to make it festive. It was special because they often invited members of the community to join in the celebrations. Especially kids from the treatment center nearby.

It should be a beautiful sight, but instead it brought sad memories. Reminders of what was, and what could have been. He could hear the sound of laughter and singing coming from the newly renovated barn hall. He should have been decorating the ranch with the love of his life—but she was gone.

He should feel the magic, but he only felt sorrow right now. He wished he could feel the magic, but that was all lost when his fiancée walked out on him. Her name was Paige. She was everything to him. He really thought he had a future with her.

He prayed to the Lord to give him strength to get over what happened, but he wondered if he'd never feel love again. His prayers seemed to go unanswered. He'd asked God to help him to forgive her what she did to him that night. Trust was always a big thing for him. Without it there was nothing. And she'd broken his trust. She left him without telling him why.

Even though she'd broken his heart and betrayed his trust. He still loved her. Missed her. Wished he could make things right with her. But that was never going to happen now. He just couldn't see himself falling in love again and trusting another woman.

Right now, the Charmings, his wonderful family, were preparing for the church Christmas play. Then in a few days, the lighting of the town Christmas tree. This time of the year seemed to keep his mind too busy to worry about anything else.

"You're not done yet?" his brother Noel teased him. "Just kidding. Looks great, cowboy."

"Thanks, bro."

"What's on your mind?" Noel asked him perceptively.

"What makes you think anything's on my mind?" Carter asked.

"Come on, cowboy? I know what you're thinking."

"And what's that?"

"That you're going to try to skip out on the annual Christmas dance."

His brother was right.

Just then his mother, Lucinda walked in cheerfully, dressed in Christmas colors, wearing one of those ugly sweaters with the reindeer lights flashing.

Carter couldn't help but grin. His mother was the town's biggest Christmas cheerleader. She'd grown the boys to love giving and sharing and to cherish the true meaning of the holiday. Sometimes the best Christmas gifts were not wrapped under the tree, but what's wrapped around the heart, the love you give to others.

"You are coming to the dance this time, aren't you, Carter?" His mother arched a brow, with a grin on her lips.

"You know, I'm not one for all that celebration, Ma."

"Oh, come on now. How else are you going to meet someone?"

"Maybe, I don't want to. I already did and it didn't work out."

"Oh, darling. You know I'm so sorry about what happened between you and Paige, but you have to move on. You know the Lord will give you beauty for your ashes."

That's what the good book said, but right now, Carter had a hard time getting over what happened to what he thought was the best relationship he ever had.

Was it something he said? Did? He just didn't get it. The rejection and abandonment left a gaping hole in his heart. He and Paige had a large engagement party. Everything seemed fine. He'd never been so close to anyone before.

What was she hiding from him?

Carter shifted his thoughts back to the present.

His mother was right. Christmas was about love, giving, remembering the birth of Jesus. But right now, he couldn't put his head around the fact that he was broken-hearted and humiliated. His pride took a beating when she dumped him before their nuptials.

And she broke up with him around the Christmas season too. A sign that maybe the holidays wasn't meant for everyone. Especially not for him.

He and Paige dreamed of having a family of their own. Three kids and a dog. A border collie rescue. They'd had it all planned out. But it didn't work out that way and he felt that he must have done something wrong to deserve that.

It took a lot out of him to be close to anyone. After all, his own family abandoned him before the Charmings adopted him as a child.

Carter was crushed to pieces.

"It's snowing pretty hard out there," Noel said. "We'd better finish up later."

The visibility decreased with each heavy snowfall. As they got ready to go back to the main house, Carter paused.

Just then his attention turned to the roadside. He saw a car in the distance.

"What are you looking at?" Noel asked.

"Do you see that?"

"See what?" Noel looked but couldn't see much.

"I could swear I saw blinkers."

"Blinkers?"

"Looks like someone's in a ditch somewhere. I'm going to go out there."

"You want me to come with you? Snow's coming down hard."

"Nah, I'll be all right."

Carter then got into his pickup truck and made his way out to the road.

Before long he came to a snowbank where he saw a blue sedan stuck. There was a woman beside the car, shivering, trying to make a phone call.

She then turned around and called out, "Charlie! Charlie!"

Her hood covered her face. Snow flurries swirled around them.

"You all right, ma'am?" Carter asked. "You need help?"

The woman wore a parker winter jacket with an oversized faux fur trimmed hood. Her face was barely visible. Long strands of ebony hair peeked through the sides of her hood as it swayed with the heavy gusts of wind.

"I'm fine," she said, then frantically shouted, "Charlie!"

"You're looking for your friend?"

"Sorry, I'm just...I was looking for my dog. He's a husky rescue. He.... he ran off from my friend's house."

"Ma'am, I'm sorry about that. I'll help you look for him. Where was he last seen?"

"I was driving around but my car's dead. So's my phone."

"I'll get someone to look at your car for you, but you really shouldn't be out here by yourself right now. Storm's going to get worse. You're in luck, you can use my phone and I'll drive you around to find Charlie."

"Thanks. I really appreciate it. Though I don't feel so lucky right now."

Carter paused for a moment. The woman's voice sounded familiar.

He liked the sound of her voice. He didn't know why. But something inside him resonated with it. She had a soft yet warm voice and strong.

Wait a minute...

It couldn't be her...

As if she read his mind, the woman lifted her hood slightly so that she could get a look at him.

The snowflakes began to let down a little, but she looked like a pretty Christmas portrait. Her lips were red like strawberries, her lovely dark hair silky and wavy, her eyes were lovely, framed by long thick lashes. She looked precious. Like a breathtaking cover model. He could tell by her hip hugging parka jacket that she still had those lovely curves. Her legs seemed to go on for ever. She wore a slim fitted pants with long leather snow boots.

But she looked mortified when their eyes met.

"Oh, my goodness! Carter!" she said, her eyes wide with surprise.

"Paige," was all he said. He didn't know what to feel right now.

Paige was there.

He never thought he'd ever lay eyes on her pretty face again. But as the snow melted on his face, so did the anger he'd felt when she walked out on him.

She smiled. "Thank you, Carter. And thanks for rescuing me out here."

"Hey, it's no trouble. I just happened to spot your flashing lights in the distance."

"You've got good vision."

Good vision?

He wished he had good vision when it came seeing into the future.

Talk about love being blind.

And speaking of blind. He knew he couldn't afford to be blindsided by his beautiful ex-fiancée again.

Carter, focus.

Okay, so he had no idea where his thoughts were going right now, but he had to do the right thing.

Carter escorted Paige to his Ford pickup truck and closed the passenger side door when she got in.

He then made his way over to the driver's side, the heavy gusts of wind moving faster and faster again, snow falling fast once more.

"We'll find Charlie." His voice was confident. He hoped he found her husky in time.

"Thanks, Carter. I really appreciate this." She bit down on her lower lip. He loved when she did that. But he had to shift his focus.

"So when did you adopt Charlie?"

Did she choose companionship with a dog instead of him?

"After Mom passed, Dad was in a state. Well, we rescued Charlie from the shelter and...well, he's been the best thing for Dad and me. He's very protective and full of energy.

"How is your dad?"

"He...he passed away."

"Man, I'm really sorry to hear that."

"Thank you. He never got over Mom passing and seeing her suffer before she died broke his heart."

"I can just imagine."

As he started the car, the engine wouldn't budge.

"What's wrong?" Paige asked.

"Everything," he said, matter-of-factly. "Looks like we're both stuck now."

Chapter 2

"I'm worried about Carter," Lucinda said to her sister Nellie as they fixed ornaments on the Christmas tree at the main house.

Nellie glanced out the window looking at the flurries of snow falling heavy outside. "Oh, don't worry. Carter's good on the road. He'll be safe."

"Oh, no not that. I know he'll be fine there. I'm just worried he's given up."

"Given up?"

"Yes. He's going to skip the annual Christmas dance again."

"Oh no."

"His father's death really hit him hard. You know Cam and Carter were inseparable. Then his fiancée broke up with him."

"Yes, that was awful."

"I know. He never got over the fact that she didn't give him a reason why she left him."

"Yes, that was terrible, wasn't it?"

"I tried to tell Carter not to give up. That the Lord will give him beauty for his ashes and that everything happens for a reason. He hasn't even been to church in a while. Carter has so much love to give. He's such a good man. I really hope he would start going out again and seeing people."

"He will. I will talk to him."

"I don't think that will help. He won't listen to anyone."

"What you need to do is get him out on a blind date. Have you ever thought of that?"

"No. And I know he won't go for it."

"Look at us two, plotting to get Carter matched up."

"Well, all my boys are single right now. I know they've had their share of heartbreak but I don't want them to give up on love."

"You know something," her sister said. "I think they just might need a little help along."

Lucinda gave her sister a sly look as she watched her thinking. She could practically see the wheels in her sister's head turning.

"You know something?" Nellie said, twirling an ornament of an angel in her hand. "I think I know what to do."

"And what's that?" Lucinda asked, taking the ornament from her sister's hand and placing it strategically on the tree.

It was a large Christmas tree, a very special tree with a special story behind it. They had just started to decorate it and it would probably take a while.

"You know sister Sue Ellen from the church?"

"Yes?" Lucinda said cautiously.

"Well, her daughter is single. She's just been through a divorce and I heard she's looking for husband number two.

"Oh, is that so?"

"Yes, that's so."

"But what do you know about Sue Ellen's daughter? I mean, is she nice? And is she honest? You know Carter has this thing about honesty. He can't deal with anyone else pulling the wool over his eyes. I mean who could blame him after what happened to him."

"I know, darling sis. Just leave the rest to me. Trust me. I'm the matchmaker of the church."

"You are?"

"Yes. I got Graham and Lilly together. Remember?"

"You did that?"

"Well, kind of. I mean they came to my rescue when I fell after that heatwave, remember. I was singing in the choir and I just collapsed from the heat."

"Oh, right. I remember, the air conditioner had broken down at the church during that heatwave."

"Exactly."

"But how did you get those two together?" Lucinda arched her brow.

"They both came to my rescue and got me into an air-conditioned car. And they stayed with me. I was out of it at the time but then they ended up talking to each other."

"Nellie!"

"What?"

Her old sister was a hoot. Sometimes. She was seventy. Ten years older than Lucinda. But she loved her big sis.

"So what do you plan to do? Faint in front of Carter and Sue Ellen's daughter?"

They both laughed. Then...

They heard a loud bang and the electricity went out.

"Oh, no."

"A blackout. Great. That's all we need."

"Now I'm really worried about Carter," Lucinda said.

"Don't worry, he'll find someone. I'll see to it."

"No. He's out there helping a stranded driver. And now it looks as if the town's blacked out." She glanced out the window frantic, seeing nothing but darkness.

"I hope he'll be okay. Anything can happen."

There was no power. Now Lucinda was about to have panic attack.

Chapter 3

Carter didn't want to worry Paige. He wanted to help her find her dog, Charlie. A surge of duty rushed through him to protect her, to help her, to keep her safe. The truth was, he never stopped caring for darling Paige. Even though she crushed his heart when she broke off their engagement over a Christmas holiday—of all time.

He moved the steering wheel to turn the tires to make them straight then he got out of the car. He could see snow accumulating faster than a speeding bull.

He cleared a path around his tires and tried to dig snow away from them. He couldn't believe how fast the snow accumulated in that short time.

Mistletoe was famous for its winter storms. That's why he always made sure he was prepared. He moved around to the back to get a shovel.

"Can I help?" Paige offered, getting out of the truck, her hair swaying in the heavy gusts of wind. She looked like a snow angel.

"Please, let me help," she offered again.

That's darling Paige for you, always willing to help.

"I'm good. Thanks for the offer though."

He was dying to ask her what she was thinking walking out on him?

Why did she leave him?

Why didn't she return any of his calls?

Did she meet someone new? Was that it?

Did the Lord bring her back to him for a reason, so he could have closure before he moved on?

She'd left to take care of her father, after her mother passed, but she never came back. She told him she would be moving back to her home city. But now she's back in Mistletoe. He had so many questions to ask her, but right now, they had other priorities like finding Charlie and getting out of the snowstorm.

Was this some sort of sign? Was the Lord trying to get Carter and Paige back together?

He didn't think so. Maybe it was just a coincidence. After all, the man upstairs knew how much he was broken by her leaving him. Maybe she was going to apologize or explain why. But he didn't want to get his hopes up.

Right now, he had to make sure he got her to safety and find her pooch.

Then maybe he'll stay away from her.

After all, this could only spell trouble, right?

She had plenty of time to call him over the past two years to let him know what the deal was, but she didn't.

He knew she was going through a lot after her mom passed, but he wanted to be there for her, to help her through it, but she wouldn't let him.

She hugged herself as she walked over to him. He could tell she was shivering slightly. He wanted to reach out and give that bear hug, like he used to give her, to let her know everything would be all right.

"Are you sure? I mean we're in this together. You saved me just now, and you're helping me look for Charlie. I want to do something."

"Okay, if you want, you can get behind the steering wheel and touch the gas when I tell you to."

"Sounds good," she said and got into the driver's side of his truck.

Just then the power in the city went out. They were pitched into darkness on the road, save for his headlights.

"Oh, no," she said after she wound down the window. "Power outage. What's going to happen now? There's no visibility."

She was right.

They were in more trouble now than before.

How were they going to get to Charlie? What were they going to do now?

Between the heavy gusts of snow and the darkness, they were in more danger if they ended up skidding into goodness knew what.

He knew during a winter storm the best advice was to stay home. Well, they were quite a ways from home right now.

He knew they had to stay warm and stay safe. He checked out his cell phone and the battery level was at five per cent.

He'd been busy all day and hadn't had a chance to charge it yet.

This was nothing. He served his time in the military. Getting out of sticky situations was his thing.

Survival was the key. Being prepared for anything was important. Carter lived by that. He was prepared for anything, well physically, not where his heart was concerned.

"Right now, we've got to keep safe," he said.

She got out of the truck and moved closer to him. He then reached over to hug her and she hugged him back.

He felt a tingling sensation down his spine, was that the cold? Or was that his feelings for Paige?

She smiled up at him. "Thank you. You feel so warm."

"No problem."

He had extra food and water in his truck, a flashlight, shovel, battery supply and some first aid supplies, and a blanket. Thank goodness for that.

Carter said a silent prayer to the man upstairs that he'd take them safely back to the ranch in this messy storm. He wished he could pray the storm away, but he knew that it was better that they stay safe. He knew storms happened all the time, especially storms in your life.

His old man once told him that the Lord could get them through any adversity, if they believed and never gave up hope.

"What should we do?" she asked, snuggling closer into him.

"You want a blanket? I've got one in the truck."

"That would be great, thanks."

He walked her back to the truck as the wind blew against them and swirling snow decreased their visibility. He held onto her to keep her steady. Once she was in the truck. He made his way into the driver's seat and closed the door shut, the wind howling around them. He then reached back for the blanket in the backseat and wrapped it around her.

"Thank you. You really are a hero in a time of need."

"Just prepared. My old man used to tell us to be prepared for anything."

"He was special, wasn't he?" she said.

"He sure was. I really miss him. Thought he'd be around forever."

Sorrow swept over Carter. Not only for the loss of his dad, but for the loss of his fiancée. For the future he thought they'd have.

If this was a sign that he could have a second chance with her at all, then it was a strange sign.

Paige looked down. He couldn't tell but she seemed as sorry as he was.

"Anyway, the best thing right now would be to stay in the truck and keep warm," he said. "I'll turn on the heat once in a while—just for 10 minutes to keep us warm, then open the window so we don't get carbon monoxide issues then shut off the engine. We'll wait until the storm dies down a bit then we can search for Charlie."

"Sounds good. I just hope he'll be all right out there." She hesitated as if she wanted to say something more. Then she stopped and looked away.

"Siberian Huskies are resilient," he added. "They can withstand the most frigid temperatures. He'll be all right. We just have to get to him."

"Thank you. You're right." She huddled up in the front seat after they switched and he sat back in the driver's chair.

She then started singing *Silent Night*. Her voice was soft and beautiful and melodic.

"You know that's my favorite song," he said, an appreciative smile curving his lips.

She turned to him and said, "I know. It's *our* favorite song. It *was* our favorite song."

"Yes, it was."

She looked into his eyes.

A sweet shiver danced down his spine.

He had to ignore those feelings. He shouldn't get his hopes up.

This was one cowboy that wasn't going to be suckered into that romance thing again. He'd vowed he'd never marry, never get involved seriously with another woman after Paige left him.

He thought they'd connected so well in the past. They looked out for each other. She was his rock and he was hers. Or so he thought.

He always wondered if she left him for another man. Was that it? Did she find someone else in her home city when she went back home to take care of her mother and then her father?

Torn.

That's how he felt right now. He sure wished the Lord would give him another sign. A clear sign on what to do now. He wanted to be angry with her. But he just couldn't. His heart melted every time she was near him.

Butterflies exploded in his belly when she brushed her hand against his, like when he handed her the blanket just a while ago. And that sweet intoxicating scent of her perfume wafted to his nostrils. He always loved her scent. He always loved everything about her. Except what she did to him two years ago. Around a Christmas holiday.

It was just a few weeks before Christmas when she broke off with him then.

She was the reason he'd stopped celebrating the holidays.

And now?

She was back. Around the holidays.

Christmas.

It was the time of year to celebrate the birth of Christ. It was also a time for family, love, good home cooking, feasts, festive celebrations, Christmas lights, snowball fights, sleigh rides in the snow, Christmas plays, dances, love in the air. And unity.

He and Paige always celebrated the holidays together. They always went all out for a fun time.

They'd sang at a Christmas concert once. His mom said they sounded like two angels in love.

Well, that was then, not now.

"What's on your mind?" she finally asked him. Her pretty eyes wide and innocent looking.

"Nothing."

"Nothing? Oh, come on now. You look like you have the world on your shoulders, Carter. I know you."

"Do you?" he asked, softly.

"Hey..."

"Sorry, I just...It's been a while, hasn't it?"

"Yes, it has."

There was that awkward silence between them. What was he going to do now?

"You left without saying a word," he finally said.

There he said it.

She turned to face him again, a look of shock on her face.

Chapter 4

"What?" Paige asked, stunned.

They both sat in his pickup as the snow fell hard outside, blanketing the town in a coat of white. The stars blinked in the dark night sky. But they weren't the only things that blinked.

Paige didn't think she heard right.

"You think I left you without saying a word? Is that what you *believe?*"

"Whoa! Wait a minute, now." Carter adjusted his cowboy hat. "I'm really sorry about what happened to your mom. That's terrible." His voice broke. "I wanted to help, but you told me to stay put."

She glanced down at her hands; heat climbed to her cheeks.

She couldn't tell him the real reason. She just couldn't. He wouldn't understand. He'd want to stay far away from her.

Truth was, she'd been miserable away from him. She missed Mistletoe. She missed the ease of the country life. The simple life. The wide-open spaces. The sweet cozy small town where everybody knew your name and they all cared about you. They welcomed you in with open arms every time. Unlike the big city. The city seemed so distant. So far away. Especially since she lost her mother and now her father.

Something terrible happened when Paige went back to Little Heart, Texas to take care of her mother and then her father.

That was the reason she had to break up with Carter.

She silently asked the Lord to forgive her for not coming clean with him right now. She also prayed for the wisdom to do what's right.

Oh, why was she so confused?

"Then," he continued. "After she passed, after the funeral, you said you needed to stay with your dad for a while to help him through it. That was two years ago. I waited for you, like you asked me to. Then I get this letter saying we should cool it off. What was that about? You even changed your phone number..."

Her stomach knotted into nerves. He was right. She hadn't been fair to him, but she had no choice.

"Carter, I..."

"Paige, what happened between us?" he asked, his voice so sweet and soft. "We were so happy together. You said we were meant to be together. We were so good together. We had so much fun whenever we were in the same room. You were my soul mate. I thought I was yours."

"You are...I mean you were..." She looked off, stung by humiliation.

He was right, and she knew it.

Should she tell him the real reason why?

Would he be upset? Would he understand?

"I *was*...?" he echoed.

"You still are, Carter. I mean...well, you know what I mean."

"No, I don't, Paige. Tell me." His voice was gentle and warm.

She paused for a moment. Her heartbeat galloped in her chest like a bucking bull at a rodeo.

"I can't tell you, Carter. I've never stopped love.... I mean, you'll always mean something to me, but we just can't be together." She turned to stare out at the falling snowflakes, so pretty against the night sky as the wind blew dancing flurries around the pick-up truck. She hoped he wouldn't press any further.

Her heart pounded hard inside her, wishing she didn't have to face him again. The last things she wanted to do was to hurt him. Again.

Carter and she could never be together and that's all he had to know. He didn't need to know the reason. Not the *real* reason.

If he ever found out about her, he wouldn't want anything to do with her.

*****Rescued by the Cowboy at Christmas Book 1 (Cowboy Under the Mistletoe) is available now.**

www.ingramcontent.com/pod-product-compliance
Lightning Source LLC
Chambersburg PA
CBHW031407160726
47993CB00003B/1134